DOGBIRD

PAUL STEWART

Illustrated by Tony Ross

www.randomhousechildrens.co.uk

For Anna

DOGBIRD

A CORGI BOOK 978 0 552 56798 5

Published in Great Britain by Corgi Books,
an imprint of Random House Children's Publishers UK
A Random House Group Company

Corgi Pups edition published 1998
This Colour First Reader edition published 2013

1 3 5 7 9 10 8 6 4 2

The Random House Group Limited supports the Forest Stewardship Council (FSC®),
the leading international forest certification organization. Our books carrying the FSC
label are printed on FSC®-certified paper. FSC is the only forest certification scheme
endorsed by the leading environmental organizations, including Greenpeace. Our paper
procurement policy can be found at www.randomhouse.co.uk/environment.

MIX
Paper from
responsible sources
FSC® C013123

Set in Bembo MT Schoolbook 21/28pt

Corgi Books are published by Random House Children's Publishers UK,
61–63 Uxbridge Road, London W5 5SA

www.**randomhousechildrens**.co.uk
www.**randomhouse**.co.uk

Addresses for companies within The Random House Group Limited can be found at:
www.randomhouse.co.uk/offices.htm

THE RANDOM HOUSE GROUP Limited Reg. No. 954009

A CIP catalogue record for this book is available from the British Library.

Printed in Italy.

Contents

COLOUR FIRST READER books are perfect for beginner readers. All the text inside this Colour First Reader book has been checked and approved by a reading specialist, so it is the ideal size, length and level for children learning to read.

Series Reading Consultant: Prue Goodwin
Honorary Fellow of the University of Reading

Chapter One

It was lunchtime. Alice Carey
was sitting at a table with her
mum and dad. The radio was
on, but the music was drowned
out by the sound of howling.

"That wretched bird is driving me round the bend!" Dad muttered.

At that moment the door burst open, and Lex, Lol and Lance – the family's three black labradors – bounded into the room and barked up at the bird-cage.

Alice's mum jumped up. As she did so, the table-cloth got caught round her leg, and the whole lot – plates of lasagne, glasses of water and orange squash, knives and forks, salt and pepper – came crashing to the floor.

"That's it!" her dad stormed.
"That bird has got to go!"

★ ★ ★

The bird in question was a
budgie. He belonged to Alice.

On her seventh birthday, her
mum and dad had taken her
to the pet-shop to choose her
very own pet. But what animal
would be best?

With Lex, Lol and Lance around, it wouldn't be fair to buy a kitten.

And Alice thought that guinea pigs were boring.

And Alice's mum refused to
have a snake in the house!

So it was that, after much
humming and haaing, Alice
chose a budgie.

"Perfect," said Mum.

"Ideal," said Dad.

It was only later that they discovered how wrong they had both been.

The pet-shop man told them the budgie was a talker. On the way home, Alice sat in the car with the cage in her lap. She tried to teach him a couple of things. *"Who's a clever boy, then?"* and *"My name's Blue."*

But by the time they pulled up outside Alice's house, the budgie hadn't said a single word.

"Wait till we get him inside," said Mum. "He'll soon find his voice then."

Mum turned the key in the
lock and pushed the door open.
Lex, Lol and Lance raced into
the hallway. Normally, they were
quiet, but the sight and smell of
the bright blue bird seemed to
drive them crazy.

Time and again they jumped
up at the cage, barking furiously.
And the budgie? Well, Alice's
mum was right. He did find his
voice. He opened his beak and
barked back at them.

"Dogbird," Dad laughed – and the name stuck.

From that moment on, life in the Carey family changed – and for the worse. For although it seemed funny at first, a barking budgie was no joke.

★

Dogbird barked at the milkman. He barked at the postman.

He barked when Alice's friends came to play. And every time he barked, Lex, Lol and Lance would join in. It drove everyone bonkers.

Woof! Woof! Woof!

Louder and louder, they
would get. The budgie and the
dogs, all barking wildly together.
Once they'd started nothing
would make them stop.

Woof! Woof! Woof!

Sometimes the dogs would escape from the kitchen into the sitting-room where Dogbird's cage hung by the window. It was then that the barking grew loudest of all. You couldn't hear yourself think.

WOOF! WOOF!
WOOF! WOOF!
Day after day, the barking
would start up. Night after night,
everyone's sleep was disturbed.
The neighbours complained.
Someone wrote to the council.

Now, six weeks later, with
the dogs jumping around in
the remains of their lunch and
Dogbird still loudly barking,
Alice's dad had finally reached
the end of his tether.

Chapter Two

Before Alice could protest, the telephone rang. It was Grandma and, from the look on her mum's face, something was wrong.

"Oh, how awful," she said.
"Stay where you are. We'll
be right over." She put the
phone down. "Grandma's been
burgled."

Alice shuddered. "Poor
Grandma," she said. "She'll
want one of my special cuddles."

"No, Alice. Not now," said her mum. "Grandma sounded in rather a state. You can play with Katie while we go and see how she is."

"We'll be seeing her again tomorrow," said Dad. "You can cuddle her then."

Alice knew there was no point arguing – at least they'd forgotten about Dogbird. At that moment, though, Lex, Lol and Lance came tearing back into the room to remind them. Their wagging tails sent everything flying. The barking was deafening!

"Not again!" Mum shouted. "Get to your baskets, the lot of you!"

"I'll tell you what," said Dad, as he grabbed the dogs by their collars. "*We'd* never get burgled. A loud dog is better than any alarm."

"And we've got three!" said
Mum.

Dogbird growled. Alice stared
at him sadly.

"Four," she said quietly.

Katie was Alice's best friend
and next-door neighbour. As
they sat together in Katie's
tree-house, Alice told her all
about the burglars.

"They took *everything*!"
she said.

"Everything?" gasped Katie.

"All Grandma's secret treasures," Alice said. She was enjoying the look of wide-eyed horror on her friend's face. "Of course," she said, "*we'd* never get burgled – because of the dogs."

Katie nodded. "I wish we had a dog," she said. "Dad says

they're too much trouble. And too noisy."

"But it's the noise that's important," said Alice. "The barking frightens the burglars away . . ."

As she spoke, the noise in question – barking – exploded from Alice's house. It was Lex, Lol, Lance and, loudest of all, Dogbird.

Katie spun round. "Burglars!" she cried.

But Alice didn't think so.
"Quick!" she cried. "Before
we're too late!"

Chapter Three

The two girls leapt down from
the tree-house, slipped through
the hole in the fence, and raced
to the back of Alice's house.

They peered in through the
window. Alice saw the dogs
leaping about, the cage on its
side – the flapping wings.

"DOGBIRD!" she screamed.
She hammered on the glass,
but the dogs took no notice.
Their game was far too much
fun.

Alice dashed to the back door, through the kitchen and into the sitting-room. When she got there, things had gone from bad to worse.

The cage door had sprung open and Dogbird was now free. He was fluttering between the

lights and the picture-rail, with
the dogs crashing about after
him.

They knocked over the coffee
table, they leapt on the settee,
they scrabbled up the wall shelves.
Books tumbled, cushions flew.
There was millet everywhere.

Crash!

Mum's favourite vase lay in pieces on the floor.

"GET TO YOUR BASKETS," Alice bellowed.

The dogs froze. The game was clearly over. Heads down and tails between their legs, they plodded back to the kitchen.

Alice slammed the door behind them and hurried to Dogbird.

Katie had stood the cage up, and Dogbird was back inside, trembling.

"Poor thing," said Alice. "Did the naughty doggies frighten you?" She turned to Katie. "It's been like this ever since I got him."

"I know," said Katie. "I live next door, remember."

"Is it **really** noisy?" Alice asked.

"Sometimes," said Katie. "It makes Dad so grumpy."

"I'm sorry," said Alice. "It's the dogs – they won't leave him alone."

Katie shrugged. "Perhaps it's not their fault."

"What do you mean?" said Alice.

"Well," she said. "What do you think a dog says when it barks?"

Alice laughed. "**Hello**, I suppose."

"Or, **Go away! I'm dangerous**!" said Katie.

"Or, **Let's play**!" said Alice.

"Exactly!" said Katie. "And
those are the things that Dogbird
is saying to them when he barks.
The dogs are only responding.
They're probably just trying to
get him out of the cage so they
can go and play."

Alice nodded. It made sense.
Trust her to end up with a
budgie that could only speak **dog**.

Chapter Four

Afterwards, neither Alice nor Katie could remember who first suggested setting Dogbird free. The idea just sort of happened, the way ideas sometimes do.

"After all," said Alice, "Dad said he'd have to go." She unhooked the cage from its stand. "Anyway, I've never liked him being stuck behind bars."

"He must get lonely on his own," said Katie. She followed her friend across the room. "In Australia, the wild ones live in flocks."

Alice sighed. "All Dogbird's
got is his reflection."

She opened the French
windows and stepped outside.
Dogbird wagged his tail
feathers.

"He can hear the call of the wild," Katie whispered.

"A bird needs to be free," said Alice. She opened the cage door. Dogbird didn't move. "I said . . . Dogbird! Get out of there."

Dogbird hopped to the end of the perch, and watched Alice through one mistrustful eye. Alice reached inside the cage. Dogbird growled and snapped at her fingers.

But Alice would not be put off.
She had decided to set Dogbird
free, and that was what she was
going to do. Quickly and gently,
she closed her hand around his
body, and pulled him from the
cage.

"There," she said, and kissed the top of his blue and white head. Katie did the same. Then Alice opened her hands and threw Dogbird up into the air.

"*Woof*!" said Dogbird, and soared off into the sunset – a flash of sky-blue.

"He did it!" Katie shouted
excitedly.

Alice nodded. There was a
lump in her throat. "Bye-bye,
Dogbird," she whispered. "Be
happy!"

They were stepping back into
the house when a sudden noise

filled the air. Horrible it was! A
stomach-churning screeching
and squawking and jabbering
– and above it all, the sound of
frenzied barking.

"Look!" Katie cried, but Alice
had already seen.

High above the treetops,
Dogbird was being attacked.
There were sparrows, starlings,
blackbirds, magpies, crows – all
ganging up on the sky-blue
intruder.

"Leave him alone!" Alice
screamed.

But it was no good. The birds
wouldn't rest until they had
driven Dogbird away. Or worse!

"It's all gone wrong," Alice
wailed, as Dogbird darted this
way and that, trying to avoid the
sharp beaks and claws.

"Dogbird!" she called. "Come back!"

As if only waiting to be asked, Dogbird barked, twisted round in mid-air and swooped down towards her. The flock of furious birds followed close behind.

"Faster," yelled Katie.

Alice stretched out her arm.
Dogbird flew closer, barking
all the while – and landed. The
other birds flew off and chattered
angrily from the tree and fence.
Dogbird shivered miserably.
There were spots of blood on his
wing.

"Now what?" said Alice sadly.
She hung the cage back on its
stand.

Katie shrugged.
Dogbird barked.
And both girls
heard the sound of
the key in the lock.

"Hello?" said Dad, surprised. "What are you two doing here?"

"And what's all this mess?" Mum demanded.

"It was the dogs," Alice explained. "They knocked the bird-cage over." Dad groaned.

Then, not wanting to tell them about trying to set Dogbird free, she asked, "How's Grandma?"

"Fine," said Mum. "But a bit worried the burglars might come back."

"She should get a dog," said Dad. "She'd feel much safer."

"She couldn't cope," said Mum. "The walks, the feeds . . ."

Alice and Katie looked at one another and grinned. That was it! That was the answer.

"What if I gave her Dogbird?" said Alice.

Mum smiled. "Perfect!" she said.

"Ideal!" said Dad.

And this time, they were right.

And so it was that Dogbird went to live with Grandma. Life in the Carey household changed again – this time for the better.

The dogs stopped barking.

The neighbours stopped complaining. And everyone finally got a good night's sleep.

As for Grandma, she was overjoyed with the budgie. He kept her company and was no trouble at all. She called him Bluey.

Alice often went to see the pair of them. She was pleased to see that the bird was happy at last. Grandma kept the cage door open so that Bluey could fly in and out as he pleased. He never tried to escape – even when the windows were open.

And being with Grandma, he soon learned to speak.

"**Pretty Bluey**," he would say. And sometimes, "**Now where have I put my glasses?**"

Best of all, he made Grandma
feel safe. Whenever the gate
clicked, or the doorbell rang,
or he heard someone prowling
around outside, Bluey would
become Dogbird again, and bark
and bark and bark.

THE END

Colour First Readers

Welcome to Colour First Readers. The following pages are intended for any adults (parents, relatives, teachers) who may buy these books to share the stories with youngsters. The pages explain a little about the different stages of learning to read and offer some suggestions about how best to support children at a very important point in their reading development.

Children start to learn about reading as soon as someone reads a book aloud to them when they are babies. Book-loving babies grow into toddlers who enjoy sitting on a lap listening to a story, looking at pictures or joining in with familiar words. Young children who have listened to stories start school with an expectation of enjoyment from books and this positive outlook helps as they are taught to read in the more formal context of school.

Cracking the code

Before they can enjoy reading for and to themselves, all children have to learn how to crack the alphabetic code and make meaning out of the lines and squiggles we call letters and punctuation. Some lucky pupils find the process of learning to read undemanding; some find it very hard.

Most children, within two or three years, become confident at working out what is written on the page. During this time they will probably read collections of books which are graded; that is, the books introduce a few new words and increase in length, thus helping youngsters gradually to build up their growing ability to work out the words and understand basic meanings.

Eventually, children will reach a crucial point when, without any extra help, they can decode words in an entire book, albeit a short one. They then enter the next phase of becoming a reader.

Making meaning

It is essential, at this point, that children stop seeing progress as gradually 'climbing a ladder' of books of ever-increasing difficulty. There is a transition stage between building word recognition skills and enjoying reading a story. Up until now, success has depended on getting the words right but to get pleasure from reading to themselves, children need to fully comprehend the content of what they read. Comprehension will only be reached if focus is put on understanding meaning and that can only happen if the reader is not hesitant when decoding. At this fragile, transition stage, decoding should be so easy that it slowly becomes automatic. Reading a book with ease enables children to get lost in the story, to enjoy the unfolding narrative at the same time as perfecting their newly learned word recognition skills.

At this stage in their reading development, children need to:

- Practice their newly established early decoding skills at a level which eventually enables them to do it automatically

- Concentrate on making sensible meanings from the words they decode

- Develop their ability to understand when meanings are 'between the lines' and other use of literary language

- Be introduced, very gradually, to longer books in order to build up stamina as readers

In other words, new readers need books that are well within their reading ability and that offer easy encounters with humour, inference, plot-twists etc. In the past, there have been very few children's books that provided children with these vital experiences at an early stage. Indeed, some children had to leap from highly controlled teaching materials to junior novels.

This experience often led to reluctance in youngsters who were not yet confident enough to tackle longer books.

Matching the books to reading development

Colour First Readers fill the gap between early reading and children's literature and, in doing so, support inexperienced readers at a vital time in their reading development. Reading aloud to children continues to be very important even after children have learned to read and, as they are well written by popular children's authors, Colour First Readers are great to read aloud. The stories provide plenty of opportunities for adults to demonstrate different voices or expression and, in a short time, give lots to talk about and enjoy together.

Each book in the series combines a number of highly beneficial features, including:

- Well-written and enjoyable stories by popular children's authors

- Unthreatening amounts of print on a page

- Unrestricted but accessible vocabularies

- A wide interest age to suit the different ages at which children might reach the transition stage of reading development

- Different sorts of stories – traditional, set in the past, present or future, real life and fantasy, comic and serious, adventures, mysteries etc.

- A range of engaging illustrations by different illustrators

- Stories which are as good to read aloud to children as they are to be read alone

All in all, Colour First Readers are to be welcomed for children throughout the early primary school years – not only for learning to read but also as a series of good stories to be shared by everyone. I like to think that the word 'Readers' in the title of this series refers to the many young children who will enjoy these books on their journey to becoming lifelong bookworms.

Prue Goodwin
Honorary Fellow of the University of Reading

Helping children to enjoy *Dogbird*

If a child can read a page or two fluently, without struggling with the words at all, then he/she should be able to read this book alone. However, children are all different and need different levels of support to help them become confident enough to read a book to themselves.

Some young readers will not need any help to get going; they can just get on with enjoying the story. Others may lack confidence and need help getting into the story. For these children, it may help if you talk about what might happen in the book.

Explore the title, cover and first few illustrations with them, making comments about any clues to what might happen in the story. Read the first chapter aloud together. Don't make it a chore. If they are still reluctant to read alone, share the whole book with them, making it an enjoyable experience.

The following suggestions will not be necessary every time a book is read but, every so often, when a story has been particularly enjoyed, children love responding to it through creative activities.

Before reading

Although *Dogbird* is a straightforward narrative, it does jump backwards and forwards in time. The first chapter includes a flashback to when Alice gets a budgie as a pet. The next chapter introduces a serious theme about Alice's grandmother being burgled. It would be a good idea to share the first three chapters and to chat about them to ensure that youngsters understand and are encouraged to read on.

During reading

Asking questions about a story can be really helpful to support understanding but don't ask too many – and don't make it into a test on what happens. Relate the questions to the child's own experiences and imagination.

For example, ask: 'What sort of pet would you choose?' and 'Can you think what Alice could do to help Dogbird?'

Responding to the book

If your child has enjoyed the story, it increases the fun by doing something creative in response. If possible, provide art materials and dressing up clothes so that they can make things, play at being characters, write and draw, act out a scene or respond in some other way to the story.

Activities for children

If you have enjoyed reading this story, you could:

- Fill in the missing letters in this sentence:

  Alice's family have three black l_____ called
  L__, L__ and L_____.

- Match the sounds with the animal or bird that
  makes them:

  WOOF   QUACK   CLUCK   PURR
  duck   cat   hen   dog

- Draw and colour a picture of a blue budgie.

- Find the words in Chapter 4 to fill the spaces in
  these sentences:

  1._____ is Alice's best friend.

  2.Alice and Katie decide to set Dogbird _____.

  3.Dogbird was attacked by sp_____,
     black_____, ___pies and c___s.

  4.Dogbird went to live with _____.

  5.Grandma called him _____.

  6.He made Grandma feel ____.

- Visit **www.rspb.org.uk** to find out about the birds that attacked Dogbird. On that website you can click on the **Birds & Wildlife** section to find the birds by name. The sparrow will be listed as 'house sparrow' and the crow as 'carrion crow'. When birds attack each other it is called 'mobbing'. You could find out more about this by doing a search for mobbing on the RSPB website.

★ ★ ★ **COLOUR FIRST READER** ★ ★ ★

by **Sainsbury's**

CERTIFICATE
of READING

My name is

_____

I have read

_____

Date

_____

ALSO AVAILABLE AS COLOUR FIRST READERS

Dog on a Broomstick by Jan Page
Great Save by Rob Childs
Happy Mouseday by Dick King-Smith
Invisible Vinnie by Jenny Nimmo
Peas in a Pod by Adele Geras
Shredder by Jonathan Kebbe
Snow Dog by Malorie Blackman
Space Race by Malorie Blackman
Super Saver Mouse by Sandi Toksvig
The Chocolate Monster by Jan Page
The Dinosaur's Packed Lunch by Jacqueline Wilson
The Frankenstein Teacher by Tony Bradman
The Ghost Teacher by Tony Bradman
The Monster Crisp-Guzzler by Malorie Blackman
The Monster Story-Teller by Jacqueline Wilson
The Troublesome Tooth Fairy by Sandi Toksvig
Too Big by Geraldine McCaughrean
Unusual Day by Sandi Toksvig
Yo Ho Ho! by Marjorie Newman